THE LIVING LIBRARY

Donald A. Shinn

This book is dedicated to my friends and fans who have stood by me in my writing career. Special thanks go out to the Garden Girls and the crew at Vegas. You know who you are, and I appreciate all of you.

Copyright © 2019

All rights reserved. This book or parts thereof may not be reproduced in any form, stored in any retrieval system, or transmitted in any form by any means—electronic, mechanical, photocopy, recording, or otherwise—without prior written permission of the publisher, except as provided by United States of America copyright law or for promotional purposes.

Cover design and creation by Donald A. Shinn

Book Design by Donald A. Shinn

PART ONE

Diana sat baking in the sun and wondering why her parents had insisted on coming to this hellhole for a vacation. Surely there had to be better places to take your daughter on vacation than this. It had all sounded good when they'd suggested it. "Let's go to the Jersey shore for the week." Visions of amusement park rides, saltwater taffy, frozen custard, and romping in the surf had filled her head. But not this.

They were staying in a small, and small may be too kind of a word to describe it, cabin with no air conditioning, and no Wi-Fi. Not only was there no Wi-Fi but no cellular signal either. With nearly all of New Jersey blanketed with cellular, only her parents could find the one small corner of the state without it. The bedroom they'd put her in was so small she could spread her arms in any direction and touch a wall. A twin mattress, that looked as if it might have been there since the cabin was first built decades earlier was wedged into the space.

"We're within walking distance of the beach," they'd said. Sure, if you're a Sherpa used to climbing Mount Everest, but not for a normal person. The nearest thing to a beach was the bay and even that was over a mile away. Her one long walk there had ended in disappointment when she'd discovered there was no beach just rotting pilings of an old pier and the place stank. A few dead fish littered the mucky shoreline and crabs could be seen lurking beneath the water ready to pinch the toes of anyone stupid enough to try to enter the water.

The real beach, with the real ocean was over three miles away. And even that was no real beach like she'd imagined, with a boardwalk and arcades and entertainment. No, it was small strip of sand, dotted with plants designed to keep the sand from blowing away, that were about as comfortable as cacti to be near.

The good news is there were no crowds. No, most people were smart enough to avoid places like this. Escaped felons were smart enough to avoid places like this.

Only people as stupid as her parents would subject someone to a place as awful as this.

"Isn't that sunshine beautiful?" asked her mother as she plopped down alongside of Diana in a chaise lounge, immune to Diana's gloom.

"Do we have to stay here the whole week?" asked Diana.

"It's good to get away from the city and experience life here at the shore. You'll miss this place when we get back home. Mark my words."

Diana swatted her tenth mosquito of the day before replying. "I'm pretty sure I won't miss this place. I've got to get up and move around a bit. Maybe find someplace to cool off for a bit. This heat is brutal."

"Your father and I are going to the Gunderson's for dinner tonight. They're having a game night for us. From what I understand they've brought a few new board games to play."

"I'll take a pass on that. Thanks all the same."

"We won't be back until late, so fix yourself a sandwich or something before you go to bed."

The Gunderson's were the only people more stupid than her parents. Not only were they also there, but they'd bought both their cabin and the one they were letting her parents use. Diana wondered how truly stupid someone had to be to buy not just one cabin in such a hellhole, but two. Not only that, but they'd bought more land nearby and were talking of tearing down the buildings that were there and building more cabins.

She slipped into her flipflops and headed down the road towards what passed for a nearby town. It was more of an intersection than a real town, but surely someplace there had to have air conditioning.

"You don't need air conditioning here," her father had said. "The ocean breeze keeps things cool." Yeah, if the mid to upper nineties was your definition of cool and it certainly wasn't Diana's. In the six days they'd endured here, there had always been a land breeze that did nothing to cool the place but brought the lovely smell of dead fish and decay from the bay into her room. Maybe if there had ever been an ocean breeze she might have felt differently, but there hadn't been.

Today was an especially brutal day. The temps were expected to peak at nearly a hundred with sixty percent humidity and still the land breeze. In the early afternoon it was already nearly unbearable and would only get worse. Her flip flops were softening in the heat and sticking to the pavement as she trudged down the narrow two-lane road towards the only real sign of civilization in the area. If there had been anyone else stupid enough to be near here, she'd have had to fear getting hit by a car as the road didn't even have any shoulders let alone sidewalks, but fortunately no one else was as stupid as them. The road didn't even show up on their GPS and had no official name, so she'd resorted to calling it Hellhole Drive. Six small buildings were at the intersection of Hellhole Drive and whatever other street was stupid enough to have been built here.

As she neared the first building her hopes were raised. A window air conditioner was humming away. She hurried to the door and saw that it was a public library and miracle of miracles, it was open. She opened the door and felt the cool air embrace her.

"Oh, thank God!" muttered Diana as the bell over the door tinkled a welcome.

"Ah, a fellow book lover," said an older woman who came out from an inner office at hearing the bell.

"More a lover of the air conditioning than the books actually," said Diana truthfully.

"It is a mite toasty out there today," said the older woman eyeing her curiously. "I don't remember seeing you around here before?"

"We're staying at one of the Gunderson's cabins."

"Ah, poor you. I'm afraid I'm not a fan of theirs."

"Welcome to my world."

"Well, you're welcome to look around, cool off, and browse the shelves. I'm afraid we don't have a huge selection of books, but as you've no doubt learned, there aren't a lot of people around here. Should you find a book you like, let me know. I'll be in the office. Just give a holler if you need anything."

"Thank you. I will."

The library was small by library standards, barely twenty feet wide and maybe fifty feet deep. A checkout desk occupied the area to the left of the front door. Magazines were on the wall to the right. Most were already several months old, and no new issues were obvious. A series of four large tables were between the front area and the bookcases. Most were empty, but one had a large tablecloth covering it and going all the way to the floor. The floor was covered in a plush carpet that felt cool and comfortable under Diana's flip flops. She slipped out of the flip flops and sighed as the coolness of the carpet melted away the heat in her feet. The cool air from the air conditioner had pooled at ground level and her feet were almost feeling chilled. It was a feeling she hadn't been sure she'd ever experience again.

She walked back towards the bookshelves with her flip flops in hand in case there was a rule against bare feet, and she needed to put them back on, but the carpet felt so cool and comfortable she dreaded the thought. The bookshelves were anything but crowded. Empty spaces were rampant, and some sections had just a few books.

"She wasn't kidding when she said they didn't have a huge selection," muttered Diana pulling down a book or two and reading the back cover. Most of the books were old to very old and she only recognized a few of the authors. Fiction books dominated the selection with a few biographies thrown in. An old set of encyclopedias and a dictionary were all the reference books available and looked about as old as the librarian. Nothing really caught her eye to read, but there was no way she was leaving here until forced to.

She let out a yawn and then looked around to see if anyone had noticed, but no one was around. She'd gotten very little sleep since coming to the shore and was on the verge of exhaustion. It was then that she looked at the table covered by the tablecloth and moved towards it. She looked under the tablecloth and saw the cool dark space there just begging her to lie down to catch a quick nap. Should she ask for permission first though? Perhaps, but what if the librarian said no. No, it was better to take her chance on being caught than not being allowed a nap at all. She slid under the table and let the tablecloth fall around her. She curled up on her side as the coolness of the carpet melted the heat from her body. The tablecloth blocked out the light and in the cool darkness she fell asleep.

Diana awoke and was confused by her surroundings, then she remembered where she was. She stretched and was about to slide out from under the table when she heard it. A faint clinking noise that seemed to be drawing nearer. There was an odd, almost groaning type sound also and the deep breaths of someone. The noises stopped just outside her table and she sat frozen wondering what to do, then she heard it. An old man's voice called out, "It's okay everyone. The coast is clear."

She peeked out from under the tablecloth and saw an old man, dressed in a suit of armor standing nearby. As she watched more people came forward from the bookshelves, stretching as though they too were just awakening from a nap. All were dressed as though on their way to a costume party of some sort.

Diana looked towards the door and waited until the knight had turned and gone back towards the bookshelves before she slid out from under the table and hurried towards the door, only to find it locked.

"I say there," said a man dressed as a king. "It looks like we have a new character joining us tonight. I don't remember seeing you here before and I'm quite sure I'd remember a lass like yourself."

An oddly dressed teen boy wearing a ruffled shirt and tights then shoved the king aside and advanced on Diana.

"Ah, what light through yonder window breaks. What is thy name fair maiden? For hearing it shall ease my cares of this world and I shall treasure it forever."

"Uh, I'm Diana."

"And I am Romeo of the Montagues. Ah, Diana. The goddess of the hunt. A name fitting a maiden so beautiful, for the sight of you has trapped my heart as a snare traps a hare. Tell me my lady, what is your story?"

"My story?"

"Forgive me for being so forward, but our nights pass quickly, and our time here is limited. I am Romeo of Shakespeare's Romeo and Juliet. You are Diana of which story?"

"I'm just Diana, I guess."

"Hmm. You are a special one. A young woman of exceptional grace and beauty. But I must know who wrote you."

"Wrote me?"

"I was written by the great William Shakespeare. A master draftsman of characters. I dare say whoever wrote you was a draftsman of nearly that caliber based on your beauty and charm alone. Who was your author?"

"No one wrote me."

"Surely, someone had to create you. Who was it?"

"My mother and father I guess."

"You guess? You truly don't know who wrote you?"

"I wasn't written, I was born."

"Not written? I don't understand."

"I'm not a character in a book. I'm just me. I'm just a person."

"I don't understand," said Romeo. "How can you not have been written?"

"I was just taking a nap under that table and when I woke up the guy in the armor was here and then everyone else came out. I tried to sneak out to avoid interrupting whatever you guys are doing but the door was locked. So, what is this, a costume party or something?"

"Oh, bloody hell," muttered the king shoving Romeo aside and looking closely at Diana before calling out. "Quixote, where the bloody hell are you man?"

"I'm here my liege," said the old knight waddling forward as his armor clanked.

"When you examined the room did you perchance look under that table?"

"I may have my liege."

"You may have?"

"I may not have also. The room was quiet, and I don't see so well these days. I assumed no one was there. No one has ever been there before."

"So," asked Diana, "who are you people anyway?"

"Forgive me my lady," said the knight. "I am Don Quixote de la Mancha. They call me the destroyer of evil. And this is Arthur. King of the Britons. Wielder of Excalibur, husband of Guinevere, and defender of the British Isles from the Saxons. You've already met the boy, pompous little twit that he is. I must apologize for his lack of manners. He seems to follow the lead of the smaller of his two brains the most."

"Enough Quixote," said the king impatiently before turning to face Diana once again. "You're human?"

"Well, yeah. Just like you guys. You are human right?"

The king pulled a chair out from under the table and plopped down upon it and sighed.

"You are human right?" asked Diana. "I mean this is some sort of a costume party or something, isn't it?"

As she looked around the room at the various people who had now filtered out, she started to realize that if these were costumes, they were much higher quality than what one typically saw. The fur on the king's outfit looked genuine as did the intricate embroidery. The armor worn by the knight looked real and not plastic. It was a bit worn but looked real enough. The long white silk robe worn by Cleopatra appeared to be made of genuine silk. The snake wrapped around her arm was alive and tasting the air with its tongue. No one was wearing sneakers or modern shoes. The jewelry that adorned the various figures appeared real and not the cheap costume jewelry one typically saw.

"How do I explain this," muttered Arthur.

"Look," said Diana. "I don't care who you guys are or what you're doing here, I just want to get back home. If you could unlock the door or show me how you got in, I'll be only too happy to leave and let you do whatever it is you're all doing. I know some people back home who are furries and that's fine. I don't care. To each their own."

"Furries?" asked Arthur.

"People who dress up like animals and have sex," said Diana. "I opened the wrong closet at a friend's house and saw his parents' costumes with shall we say oddly placed openings. It's all a bit weird to me, but it makes them happy, so whatever. What you guys are doing looks a bit weird to me too, but hey, whatever makes you happy. I just want to go home. Can someone unlock the door or show me another way out?"

"I'm afraid there is no other way out," said King Arthur.

"But how did you all get in? You weren't here a while ago."

"We live here," said Don Quixote. "This is our home. We only leave when we're checked out and then we're brought back later. The only way to leave here is to be checked out."

"Checked out?" asked Diana warily.

"It's different for us than you," said Arthur. "You're not like us."

"What do you mean?"

"You exist at all times in this world," said Arthur. "We don't. We only come out on occasion, typically when no one else is around. But my friend here, overlooked you. You should have never seen us."

"I'll be only too happy to forget I ever saw anything if you can just show me the way out."

"My lady, the door is the only way out for you," said Arthur. "The windows were sealed after Superstorm Sandy. They are now unbreakable and cannot be opened. You say the door is locked? Can you not unlock it?"

"I don't have a key. Who are you people? I mean really?"

"You were born of humans, were you not?"

"Well, yeah, if you call my parents human. I have doubts sometimes."

"It took nine months for you to emerge in human form. We are born in a similar manner, well not really, but suffice to say for us to emerge in human form takes much longer. Fifty years or more for most of us. And unlike you, we can revert back to our written state."

"Written state?"

"Allow me to show her my liege," said Don Quixote. He hurried back to the bookshelves and returned with a book in his hands. "This is where I live," said Don Quixote setting the book down on the table before her. "Allow me to demonstrate."

As Diana watched he opened the book and then seemed to melt into the pages of the book. She gasped in shock and then watched wide-eyed and open-mouthed as he emerged once again and returned to human form. Diana backed away from the table and only stopped when she collided with the rack of magazines, knocking several to the floor.

"That might have been too soon to demonstrate how we live," said Arthur. "Calm down child. We mean you no harm."

"What are you?" screamed Diana as Arthur approached her. "Are you real?"

"As real as we can be," said Arthur.

"Can I touch you?"

Arthur looked confused by this and said, "I'm afraid I don't know. We don't typically interact with humans. Why don't you try?"

He held out his arm and Diana tentatively reached out a finger to touch his hand before stopping and asking, "I won't get sucked into a book or anything will I?"

"I would assume not," said Arthur, "but there's only one way to know for sure."

Diana hesitated for a second then reached out and quickly poked the back of his hand with a finger before quickly withdrawing it. She then reached forward once more and felt the fur and velvet of the cuff on his coat.

"Okay, you're real enough then, I guess. You can all just pop into and out of books?"

"Only the ones in which we're written. To interact with others, we must leave our books and meet them here. It's why we came out tonight, to mingle among ourselves. It gets a bit boring being stuck in a book with the same characters decade after decade. Here we can meet new characters and hear their stories. When I saw you, I just assumed you were a new character."

"And you're really King Arthur? He's really Don Quixote? That's really Romeo? And she's really Cleopatra?"

"As we were written," said Arthur.

"I may just be losing my mind. I wonder if this is what a heat stroke feels like?"

"I suspect your mind is just fine," said Arthur. "You're just experiencing something new and a bit unexpected."

"Yeah, I'm not so sure about that. I'm leaning more towards me going insane."

"I can help with that," said Don Quixote. "Just wait there a moment." He returned from the bookcases a few seconds later leading an older man in an old-fashioned business suit towards her.

"This is Dr. Freud," said Don Quixote. "He's helped me tremendously. I had all kinds of anxiety issues after the authorities burned my books, but Dr. Freud has helped me deal with my issues. He's the best person to assure you that you're not insane or help you if you are."

"Sigmund Freud?" asked Diana incredulously. "But, he's real, not a character in a book."

"His biography is here so he's here," said Don Quixote. "He's a very smart man. He can help you. He's done wonders for me."

"You've heard of me then child?" asked Dr. Freud. "I'm not surprised. No doubt everyone has. I dare say there are millions of young Sigmund's in your world these days with parents naming their children after me."

"Not so much," said Diana.

"What do you mean?"

"You're like the only guy named Sigmund I've ever heard of."

"I'm the only one? How can that be?" asked Sigmund collapsing into a chair and looking shocked.

"It's just not that popular of a name."

"Still? I was teased to death as a child because of my name. I fought through it and overcame it all to make the name garner respect and now no one uses it?"

"I'm afraid not, and no offense, but none of this is making me feel any saner. I'm now talking to a dead shrink?"

"Shrink?"

"It's slang for a psychologist or psychiatrist. You know, like a head shrinker."

"This is what my profession has come to? We are viewed as head shrinkers?"

"I'm sure you do good work," said Diana trying to reassure him. "I know a few people who have been helped by psychologists. I'm pretty sure I'll need one if this isn't all some crazy dream. Is this a dream? Would I know if it was a dream?"

"Perhaps a nightmare if what you say is true," said Dr. Freud. "No one names their children Sigmund?"

"Afraid not. And I can't believe I'm really asking this of a dead guy from a book, but am I sane?"

"No one is truly sane. We're all insane, just in varying degrees. You seem sane enough to me. I've got to go and think about what you've said. You'll have to excuse me."

Diana watched as Dr. Freud walked back into the bookcases and disappeared.

"He said you were sane," said Don Quixote with a smile. "Problem solved."

"Yeah. A long dead guy just emerged from a book and said I was sane. Somehow that's not especially reassuring. And it doesn't solve the problem of me being locked in a library."

"What we have here is a quest. Arthur loves quests. The quest to free fair Diana from the library! Where should we start?"

"Perhaps finding a key would be a good idea," suggested Diana. "Or maybe a phone so I could call someone, like a mental ward to come pick me up."

"I don't know what a phone is," said Arthur. "But we could search for a key. There could be one lying around here someplace."

"Yeah, let's do that then," said Diana.

"I'm afraid I'll need someone to hold my asp if I'm to help in the search," said Cleopatra. "I'd recommend being a bit careful though, he's been a bit nippy lately, the silly boy."

"You know what, we're fine without you," said Diana. "You just keep your asp and we'll see if we can find a key ourselves. It shouldn't be that hard. There's the checkout desk and inner office. If there's a key here it should be in one of those two places."

A quick search of the checkout desk revealed no key and the office door was locked preventing them from getting into the office.

"Great, just great," muttered Diana. A quick look around confirmed the windows were all sealed tight and there was no back door. "So, I'm trapped here?"

"Don't think of it as a trap, my lady," said Don Quixote, "but as an adventure."

"An adventure? How is this an adventure?"

"You can call upon some of the greatest characters that have ever existed and hear their stories from their own mouths. Before you right now are Arthur, King of the Britons, Cleopatra, Queen of the Nile. My humble self, and that impetuous boy who seems ruled by his hormones. Have you no questions for us?"

"Questions?"

"Surely there must be something you'd like to ask us?"

"Okay," said Diana after pausing for a few seconds and looking around. She nodded towards Cleopatra and asked, "So, what's with the snake?"

"My asp is my most loyal servant."

"Servant?"

"My story is not so odd. It's probably very similar to your own. I was born to King Ptolemy the twelfth and my mother. When I was eleven, we were exiled from Egypt and lived on the outskirts of Rome where my father tried to rally support to regain his throne. We returned to rule Egypt when I was fourteen. Mark Antony and I first met then. Oh, he was a handsome man. I instantly had a bit of a crush on him.

My father died when I was eighteen and I became the queen. Things got a bit messy as my brother, Ptolemy the thirteenth and I were technically co-rulers and I was briefly married to him, but let's not dwell on that. It was something of a tradition at the time. I seized power from him however as he was a bit of an idiot. He didn't take this well and went to war against me. Things weren't going so well for my side, so I fled to Thebes for a bit of a respite.

"Things got kind of messy for my brother about then also. You see Julius Caesar was fighting a civil war with Pompey and had nearly won when Pompey fled to my brother for sanctuary. Well my brother, I did mention he was a bit of an idiot did I not? Well, he had Pompey beheaded and his head embalmed and delivered to Caesar. He hoped it would make Caesar his ally. It turned out this made Caesar a bit cross and he demanded that my brother disband his army and he and I reconcile.

"My brother didn't want to disband his army however and marched towards Caesar in a show of force. I'd heard that Caesar was fond of noble women with a fair face and body, so I went to see him in person. Mind you, that was a bit tricky. I had to be smuggled in wrapped in a bed sack, but one does what one must. Suffice to say we hit it off well and my poor old brother came out on the short end of things. My brother was arrested, his army disbanded, and he was once again forced to co-rule with me.

"Others didn't think this was such a good idea and felt that I'd unduly influenced Caesar's decision to return me to power. Caesar and I were soon under attack and forced to withstand a siege of our palace for a while. Caesar's reinforcements then showed up and drove off my brother who drowned while trying to flee. I kept a low profile at the time what with being pregnant with Caesar's child and all and him being married to Calpurnia. Our son Caesarion then entered the picture.

"Caesar then got called away to fight another war but left me with enough troops to ensure that I'd stay in power. Once things had settled down a bit he returned to Rome and I dropped by to visit with him there. Caesar was assassinated while we were there and I'd hoped that our son would be named his heir, but it went to his grandnephew Octavian instead. Ptolemy the fourteenth was now my co-ruler, but I never liked the boy, so I had him poisoned. Then my son, my dear Caesarion became my co-ruler with me.

"To make a long story short, around this time Mark Antony returned to Egypt and we became quite close. Sadly, he ended up marrying Octavia and having two children with her and abandoned me for a bit, but I managed to woo him back and we had twins of our own. Things were a bit off and on after that. Antony named Caesarion the official heir to Caesar which didn't go over so well in some quarters. Another war broke out, and Antony committed suicide rather than surrender. I was to be sent to Rome and paraded through town as a captive and frankly, I didn't want to go, so I used my asp friend here to save me the trouble and end my life.

"As you can see, it's a story probably not unlike your own."

"Except in every way possible," muttered Diana. "You were married to your brother?"

"It was kind of a tradition at the time. It didn't really mean all that much to either of us."

"And you used your snake to kill yourself?"

"I'd tested multiple poisons on various prisoners and the snake venom seemed both the most effective and least traumatic. Those bitten just more or less drifted off into sleep and never awoke. Some of the poisons at the time were much, much worse with horrible suffering coming before the death. Would you like to hold my asp?"

"Uh, no. But thanks all the same," said Diana. She turned to face Romeo and said, "I think I already know Romeo's story."

"Do you now then?" asked Romeo.

"But where's Juliet?"

"Still in her book I'm afraid," said Romeo. "But her absence gives us an opportunity to get to know one another better."

"Aren't you supposed to be a one-woman kind of man who dies for Juliet?"

"Hah!" laughed Cleopatra. "He's wooed every woman and half the men here. The boy has no loyalty to anyone. You should have seen him the first time he saw Helen of Troy. My god, he nearly trampled me to get to her."

"So, you and Romeo then?" asked Diana.

"We had a thing. It didn't last long. Nothing lasts long with Romeo outside of his book. Suffice to say, he doesn't stay true to his character."

"Helen of Troy had a face to launch a thousand ships," said Romeo. "What chance does any man's virtue have against such beauty."

"It wasn't her face he was staring at though," muttered Cleopatra. "Suffice to say his eyes were focused a bit lower. And don't even ask how he responds when Lady Godiva comes out to play. The boy's man parts are like a compass needle pointing to any woman in sight."

"My dear Lady Godiva is a most ravishing creature," said Romeo. "Even the virtuous King Arthur himself has been known to stare in awe upon her form."

"But poor Juliet," asked Diana, "what about her?"

"She comes out to play from time to time," said Cleopatra. "She's not necessarily so pure herself. There was a time when…"

"Don't mention that being in my presence!" shouted Romeo.

"I'll mention whoever I want silly boy," said Cleopatra as Romeo stomped off. "Juliet's got a bit of a dark side to her and likes bad boys. She's been known to associate with Jack the Ripper on occasion. She seems to like to live rather dangerously."

"Jack the Ripper comes out of his book?"

"He comes out from time to time. Most of the characters who emerge behave themselves well, but you never know what a character will do. Jack and Juliet will often hang out in the romance aisle and have some fun. I've stumbled upon them there a few times. She's not nearly as pure as she's written. The girl has a serious dark side to her for someone so young. The things they do together, well, let's just say you don't want to be included in their scenes."

"I really am losing my mind, aren't I? I mean this is crazy. I'm talking to Cleopatra about Jack the Ripper and Juliet having an affair. Sane people don't do that."

"I'm afraid I don't know what sane people do," said Don Quixote. "I've been ruled insane myself more times than I like to remember. The good doctor said you were sane however and that's good enough for me. He's a very wise man."

"I've got to figure out a way out of here."

"There could very well be a key in the locked office if only we could get to it," said Arthur.

"Yeah, if not a key then maybe there's a phone in there I could call someone for help. Let me take a closer look at that door."

Diana walked over to the office door with Don Quixote, Arthur and Cleopatra following her. A sudden squeal and the sound of a slap showed Romeo had rejoined them and been following a bit too closely behind Cleopatra for her liking.

"Is everything okay?" asked Diana looking back at the two.

"Someone's hand simply roamed where it shouldn't have," said Cleopatra. "A lesson in respect was given. It wasn't the first time and I dare say it won't be the last."

"You liked it once," said Romeo in defense.

"Once long, long ago, but not now. I know where you've been since then."

"Where?"

"Do you remember Fantine?"

"From les Miserables? Ah, yes. The virtuous Fantine. Well, she was once."

"And her friends? They all came out looking for you one night after comparing notes on you. We were barely able to keep them from burning your book and you in it."

"She is something of a fiery one. Perhaps I should pull their book down once more and pull out one or two of them."

"Yes, go do that and leave us be for a bit."

Diana watched as Romeo sauntered off towards the bookshelves.

"Should I know who Fantine is?" asked Diana.

"She was a factory worker who lost her job when evil rumors spread about her. To stay alive and support her child she had to turn to a life of prostitution. A sad story really. Lovely girl though. She pops out from time to time as do the girls she worked with. They all thought Romeo was only romancing them individually. Once they came out and started to compare notes, well things got a bit intense."

"Okay then," said Diana.

She stopped at the office door and tried the doorknob once again, but it was locked. She rattled and shook it and was about to give up when she noticed something. The hinges were on the outside of the door and had a removable pin. She tried to remove the pin using a fingernail but could barely budge it.

"I need something to pry these pins loose," muttered Diana.

"Excalibur is at your service," said Arthur removing his sword from its sheath. "Stand aside and I'll shall remove those pins in a heartbeat."

He wedged the blade under the head of the hinge pin and slid it upwards nearly an inch then swung Excalibur in a mighty arc, knocking the pin free and up to the ceiling where it bounced off before crashing to the floor. The second pin followed in a similar fashion. Arthur then placed Excalibur in the crack between the door and the hinge side and wedged the door free where it crashed to the floor.

"And the room is yours my lady," said Arthur lifting the door from the floor and setting it aside.

"Thanks," said Diana as Arthur sheathed Excalibur once more. She hurried into the small office and looked first for a phone, but there was none. She then sat behind the desk and started to rummage through the desk drawers looking for a key to unlock the front door, but there was no key. A couple of filing cabinets came to her attention next and she searched through them but found only library records and no key.

"Oh, crap!" muttered Diana as she collapsed in the desk chair.

"Fear not my lady," said Don Quixote. "All is not lost. We shall find a way to get you free. A few minutes ago, you could not enter this office, and all seemed lost, but we got you in. If we could get you into this office, we can surely get you out of this building."

"How?" asked Diana.

"There is always a way. Fear not. We will think of something."

Diana led the way back to the main section of the library. The sounds coming from the bookshelves made it clear that Romeo had found someone who was a willing partner.

"Is he always like that?" asked Diana.

"I'm afraid so," said Cleopatra. "Sadly, he lacks endurance, so you won't have to hear him for long."

A couple of loud gasps then came from the bookshelves followed by a sigh.

"As I said, he lacks endurance," said Cleopatra with a wink. "Now, had that been Davy Crockett, we'd be hearing it all night. The man is most definitely not lacking in endurance."

"You've been with Davy Crockett?"

"A time or two, but truth be told, he wears me out. I try to avoid him now unless I'm feeling especially energetic."

"So, you can all have sex with one another?"

"If we choose to. Many don't choose to. In fact, some characters almost never come out at all. They're happy in their pages and see no need to come out. Others are out all the time."

"And you don't get pregnant or anything?"

"Not unless it's been written that we do. There are chapters in my book where I'm very pregnant. If I were to come out from one of them, you'd see me vastly differently."

"Wait, what?"

"How we appear depends on what page of the book we come out from. In Dr. Freud's biography for example, Don Quixote could have pulled him out as a boy, a young man, or the more mature doctor. They're all in there. It's just a question of which one comes out."

"Can you be out in more than one form at a time?"

"No, only one version of us can exist outside the book at a time. I tend to come out in this form. I'm most pleased with my appearance from this particular chapter, so that's the chapter I use."

"You do look lovely."

"Thank you. You're most kind. This is the look I used when I was seducing Julius Caesar. It proved most effective, so I use it when I come out."

"You said Don Quixote pulled Dr. Freud out?"

"Indeed. Don Quixote has mastered a technique that few of the rest of us have mastered. He can pull someone from a book whether they wish to come or not. For the rest of us we must find who we want on a page and then ask them to join us. Some do, some don't, but Don Quixote can pull them from the page whether they wish to come or not."

"That's weird. Of course, all of this is more than a little weird. I still think I might be dreaming."

Diana then felt a firm slap across her bottom and turned around to see Arthur smiling at her holding Excalibur that he'd apparently just spanked her with. He asked, "If you were dreaming would that have not awakened you?"

"Ow! Yeah, it would have, but a simple pinch would have sufficed. That hurt!"

"I'm sorry my lady, but you wondered if you were dreaming or not. I can assure you, you're not. Would you like me to prove it again?" he asked as he pulled back the sword once more with a smile on his face.

"No!" shouted Diana. "Once was enough. I believe you."

Arthur then sheathed Excalibur again as Diana rubbed her bottom.

"It's just that this is all so strange."

"It's strange for all of us at first," said Arthur. "For fifty, sixty, sometimes seventy or more years, you live trapped within the pages of your book. Never seeing anyone else but the other characters in your book. Then suddenly one day you find you can leave the book. It's terrifying at first, but then the fascination of meeting new characters, hearing their stories and telling them your story makes it all worthwhile."

"How do you know when you can leave your book?"

"Don Quixote knows. I'm not sure even he knows how he knows, but he does. The first time any of us leave our book we're pulled out by him. It takes time to learn to do it ourselves. That first time is very strange."

"I can imagine. And you don't let people see you?"

"It is forbidden."

"Why?" asked Diana.

"Here comes Don Quixote back. Ask him."

"Ask me what my liege?" asked Don Quixote.

"Why is it forbidden to let people see you?" asked Diana.

"It isn't meant to be. We each have our own world. We should not interact. It has been that way since shortly after the first character leapt off a page."

"Who was the first character to leap off a page?" asked Diana.

"I truly do not know. It was well before my time. But what I've heard is that it was a character from the Old Testament and was more common then. Have you read the Old Testament?"

"Some of it."

"Did people back then live longer than they do now?"

"Some did. I believe some lived seven hundred years or more."

"Immortality doesn't come to humans. You all have a finite lifespan. Only the written word survives that long or longer. Those who lived that long were likely characters who moved from the written word to your world and back again, appearing long-lived in the process. But they disrupted the way things should be and soon enough it was decided that the two groups must be kept separated. It has been this way since that time. Until today anyway. I fear I may be in some trouble as a result of my oversight earlier."

"In trouble from who?" asked Diana.

"Whoever gives us this power to do what we do."

"The gods themselves give us this power and it's best not to offend the gods," said Arthur. "In this case it was an oversight and I suspect they will be merciful. Our gods are most kind and benevolent."

"I see," said Diana. "I'm still thinking I might just be going crazy or that this is a dream, but I'm getting hungry and I've never been hungry in a dream before, or maybe I have, and I just don't remember. That tilts things rather heavily in favor of me going crazy."

"You're hungry then?" asked Don Quixote. "Dear me, I fear I've been a most ungracious host. What would you like to have for a meal?"

"I don't know, but there's no food here," said Diana. "My parents were eating with the Gundersons, so I was just planning on making a sandwich or something."

"Stay there," said Don Quixote. "I'll be right back."

"As if you had anyplace else to go," said Cleopatra with a smile.

"Do you eat here?"

"We can eat, drink, smoke, we can do pretty much whatever a character in one of our books does. We can take things from our books and share them with others here on the outside also. But we don't have to. We don't feel hunger or thirst."

Don Quixote came back with a large book in his hands and escorting a young woman.

"Lady Diana," said Don Quixote. "This is Miss Eliza Leslie, and this is her New Cookery Book. She's an excellent chef who will fix you any dish you find in the cookbook. All you need do is select what you'd like."

"Fix it how?" asked Diana. "There's no kitchen here and no food here."

"Everything I need is in the book," said Miss Leslie.

"Seriously?"

"She's very good," said Arthur. "I've enjoyed many a meal she's prepared."

"Okay then," said Diana opening the cookbook and leafing through it. The recipes all looked more than a bit odd, but what wasn't odd about this day?

"Does anyone have a recommendation?" asked Diana after a few moments.

"I recently had her beef steak pie and it was delicious," said Arthur. "I highly recommend it."

"Fine by me," said Diana. "I guess I'll have the beef steak pie."

"Thank you, my lady," said Miss Leslie taking the cookbook and leafing through to find the right recipe. "It shall be here soon."

Diana watched in amazement as she melted into the book and then almost immediately emerged with a heaping plate of food that she set on the table in front of Diana along with a setting of silverware.

"Seriously?" asked Diana as the delicious scent wafted into her nose. "I can eat this?"

"Of course," said Miss Leslie. "Let me know how you like it. Oh, dear. Let me get you a drink also. Will lemonade suit your tastes?"

"That would be great," said Diana tentatively taking a forkful of the food and sniffing it. She looked at the others who were all watching her and nodding their heads in encouragement and then opened her mouth and took in the food. She was almost expecting it to turn to dust in her mouth and choke her, but it didn't. In fact, it was among the most delicious food she'd ever tasted. She quickly reloaded her fork and took a second bite. Miss Leslie had now climbed back from the book with a pitcher and a glass and poured her a cold drink of lemonade.

"Is everything okay?" asked Miss Leslie.

Diana took a couple of swallows before replying. "It's better than okay. It's perfect. This may be the best thing I've ever eaten."

"Excellent!" said Miss Leslie. "If no one needs anything else, I'd best be getting back then. You know where to find me." She then melted back into her book and Don Quixote returned the book to the proper shelf.

Diana ate until she could hold no more and then slid back from the table and sighed.

"I'm beginning to think I like being crazy if the food is this good."

"The food, the drink, there is much to be thankful for in our world," said Arthur. "We do have an advantage though in that we can't gain weight. We stay as we were written. I fear you may not share that advantage."

"If I ate like that all the time that door wouldn't be wide enough for me to squeeze through, but it was too good not to eat it."

"While you were eating, I examined the front door to see if we could perhaps pop it off its hinges, but alas, the pins, if there are any, are hidden on that door. I fear that without the key you're trapped here until morning. Will your family be worried about you?"

"If they realize I'm missing. They may not even check my room though. I think part of the reason they brought me here was so I couldn't get into any trouble. God knows there's nothing to do here. They'll probably just assume I'm in bed and go to bed themselves."

"I just wish we could get that door open for you."

"Speaking of doors," said Diana. "We probably should replace that office door. The librarian would be a bit confused to find it off the hinges in the morning. I think I'll take one more look around the office first though in case I missed anything."

She went back and started to look through the drawers once more, then while moving papers around on the desk a name caught her attention. It was Mr. Gunderson's name. She examined the paper and saw that it was a purchase agreement for the library and its contents. Was this one of the buildings he was planning to tear down? And, if so, what was to happen to the books?

"Is everything all right?" asked Arthur watching Diana from the doorway.

"Yeah, I think so," said Diana. "There's no key here. Let's get that door back in place."

"As you wish. If you could guide the far side into place, I'll set it back on the hinges and we'll hammer home the pins once more."

Diana guided the locking cylinder back into its place and then watched as Arthur slid the door back onto the hinges and inserted the pins. A tap from the hilt of Excalibur soon had the pins firmly reseated and the door looked as it had originally.

Diana now walked back towards the table and asked, "How many of you do you suppose there are here?"

Arthur shrugged and said, "Thousands, perhaps tens of thousands. Most books have a few central characters, but then there are other characters who come and go through the book. The number could be even higher."

"How many books are here?" asked Diana.

"Don Quixote knows that number," said Arthur. "He's read them all at one time or another."

"Indeed, I have," said Don Quixote. "And to answer your question, there are one thousand six hundred and fifty-seven books here all total. And the characters range from the kindest, most gentle imaginable, to the most vile and despicable imaginable."

"And you can pull them all from the pages?" asked Diana of Don Quixote.

"Only those books that have been in print long enough. It takes time, typically fifty years or more for the characters to mature enough to emerge. Of the books here only a few hundred are now ripe for the plucking. New characters emerge all the time though."

"And what if one doesn't want to go back into the book they came from? Can you force them back in?"

"I can and have had to on a few occasions. But those occasions are very few I'm pleased to report. Most know how things are done and obey the rules."

"Could I meet more characters?" asked Diana.

"Indeed, you can. Who would you like to meet?"

"I have no idea."

"Let's take a walk along the shelves then and see what catches your eye."

Don Quixote led her to the first aisle, and she saw an old copy of Peter Pan.

"I've never read the book, but I like the movies of Peter Pan. Have you met him here?"

"I have my lady. He's an odd young man. I found him a bit off-putting to be honest. Quite immature and child-like in an annoying way."

"Could he truly fly?"

"Not in this world, no. But in his book, he can."

"So, special abilities don't move from the pages?"

"I'm afraid not. If they did Arthur could simply summon Merlin to open the door for you to allow you to leave. What powers we have in our books stay there and only our characters emerge into this world."

The next book she recognized was Frankenstein's. She pulled it from the shelf and leafed through a few pages.

"Does he ever come out?"

"Rarely, I'm afraid. I've tried to get Dr. Freud to help him overcome his anxiety and fearfulness, but the other characters that are out when he emerges get scared of him and then he gets upset and retreats to his book. He's a nice enough fellow though, just not very communicative."

"I'm not sure I'd ever think of Frankenstein as being nice."

"He's had a hard life what with being pieced together from corpses and brought back to life from the dead. He's not an especially attractive fellow and he sorely lacks confidence, but he's never done any harm when he's been out. He's just skittish."

"Does anyone do harm while they're out?"

"Not really. Most of the worst characters aren't bad all the time and can behave themselves. If one is truly horrid all the time, they wouldn't make an especially good character. It is that fight between good and evil within a character that gives it depth. Those who choose to emerge, and even those I summon out, tend to behave quite well given the chance. In fact, some of those one would assume to be monsters are among the most civilized and polite while out while others who you'd expect to be more proper, like Romeo as you've seen, can be quite boorish."

"Dracula?" asked Diana pulling down yet another old book.

"Very charming. Quite nice looking also. You may wish to talk to Cleopatra about him. They had quite a thing going for a while."

"It sounds like she's pretty popular and outgoing."

"As she is in her book. What she didn't tell you in recapping her story was that when Caesar left his army behind to ensure she retained power, an equal number were enlisted to ensure she bedded no one in Caesar's absence."

"How do you know that?"

"Caesar told me himself on one of his visits. Lovely man by the way. You can see why he was a ruler. There's just power and magnificence oozing from the man. I'd follow him into battle on any day."

"And what's your story?" asked Diana. "I've heard your name, but I'm afraid I don't know much of your story."

"I was born Alonso Quixano. Books and reading were a passion of mine then, just as they are to this day. So much so that I became lost in my books. I slept little and read much. My favorite books were the chivalric romances of the time, where knights always stayed true to their word and were the champions of the downtrodden. I soon started to believe that I was such a knight and donned armor and rode the countryside righting evil wherever I found it.

"Ah, but evil was powerful, and I was a mere mortal man. In a fight to defend the honor of my dear Dulcinea, I was beaten so badly that I lost consciousness. I was taken back to my home and while unconscious nearly all my beloved books were taken from me and burned. They hoped that this would weaken my resolve, but I fear it had the opposite effect. An evil wizard then sealed the door to my library preventing access to the few books that had survived.

"But I was not to be so easily swayed by evil. I pretended to give up my quest to roust evil, hoping it would turn its gaze from me and it did. I then resumed my quest. I fought giants and enchanters and scored many great victories and a few small defeats. Sadly, I was once again enchanted by sorcerers and caged and forced to return to my home.

"Still I would never admit defeat and despite trickery of a like unseen in human history, I fought to the end to defend my dear Dulcinea. It is said that in the end I regained my sanity and apologized for what I'd done. But in truth, I had no regrets, even to this day. I could choose to emerge as the supposedly sane version of my character, but he is a fraud. The real Don Quixote is a gallant and chivalrous knight determined to root out evil wherever he finds it, so that is the character I bring out."

"You became lost in your books?"

"Are you not a reader?" asked Don Quixote.

"Not so much," said Diana.

"Ah, then you do not understand how things work. Time doesn't matter when you're lost in a book. Hunger and thirst are forgotten. Pain is forgotten. All that matters is the book. As you consume the words in the book, they also consume you. You become one with the book. When you turn that last page and read those last words, it is as though a part of you dies, yet you still live. A world that you'd lived in, for a few hours or days has ended and you find yourself back in the world you knew before, and more often than not the world you knew before is inferior in every way to the one you lived in while in the book. Getting lost in a book is the easiest thing in the world for many of us."

"I'm thinking I should maybe start reading more."

"There is nothing better."

The pair walked among the bookshelves pulling down books from time to time as Don Quixote explained the stories and the characters. From time to time he'd pull out an interesting character to meet her. Often it would be a relatively minor character whose story had intrigued him. In the course of the next few hours she met knights, and kings, peasants and servants. Ladies of every type were introduced including those of ill repute. She heard stories that enchanted her and some that scared her. Some characters made her laugh while others had her in tears hearing their story. Then the tour was nearly done. Only a few books remained.

Diana pulled one from the shelves and read the title. "The Biography of Harry Houdini."

"He is a conjurer my lady. Said to be among the best of his time."

"He's more than that," said Diana excitedly. "He was also a master lock picker. It's said he could unlock any lock."

"Including the one on the door here?"

"I would hope so. Can you pull him out for me?"

"It would be my pleasure. I've never met the man myself. I don't think he's ever come out, so he may be a bit confused at first, but he appears ripe to leave. If you'd stand back a bit, I'll extract him from the book."

Diana backed away and watched in fascination as Don Quixote leafed through the book and then settled on a page. His hand reached into the book and then came out clutching another person's hand and soon the whole body of Harry Houdini was out and standing near Don Quixote.

"Where am I?" asked Harry.

"You're among friends," said Don Quixote. "I've just plucked you from your book."

"Are you okay?" asked Diana, happy to see someone who looked as confused as she felt.

"I believe so," said Harry flexing his fingers and wrists and taking a few tentative steps. "This is most bizarre."

"I'm glad someone else feels that way," said Diana. "I was beginning to think it was just me."

"Were you plucked from a book also?" asked Harry.

"No, I just fell asleep under a table and woke up to find myself here."

"And, where are we?"

"This is a small library at the Jersey shore. I'm kind of locked inside and we were hoping you might be able to help me escape. You are an escape artist."

"I'm alive then?"

"Indeed," said Don Quixote. "I plucked you out a page before you were to die."

"You plucked me from a page before I was to die?"

"This is your book," said Don Quixote holding up the biography. "This is where you typically live. I just pulled you out to see if you could help Diana. I wanted you at your most mature and experienced, so I plucked you out the page before you were to die."

"This is madness. Have I lost my mind?"

"See?" said Diana, "It's not just me."

"You haven't lost your mind. It just takes a bit to adjust to this reality. You live within the words of your book and among the other characters in your book. If the book survives, you survive with it."

"I dedicated my career to exposing false mystics and their lies, yet here I find myself facing a reality, if it is a reality, quite unlike anything I'd imagined possible. You say I'm dead in the real world then?"

"I'm afraid so."

"I should reach out to my wife. I promised to try and communicate with her from beyond the grave."

"She's probably dead also," said Diana. "It's been a while. You died about a hundred years ago."

"I could bring her from the book if you'd like to talk to her again," said Don Quixote. "It won't take a minute."

"That would be good," said Harry watching as Don Quixote then leafed through the book to find a page with Harry's wife on it and then reached into the book and pulled her from the book.

"Bess?" said Harry upon seeing his wife emerge. "Is that really you?"

"Harry?" asked Bess and the two embraced in a deep hug and kissed.

"What madness is this?" asked Bess when she looked around the space.

"We are apparently now characters in a book who can be summoned by this one at will." He nodded towards Don Quixote.

"Given time you'll learn to emerge on your own also," said Don Quixote. "It's not so hard. Once you know you can do it, that's half the battle. Most characters just don't know they can do it."

"Why are we here?" asked Bess.

"I kind of need someone to unlock that door for me," said Diana. "I know your husband can pick locks, so we pulled him out, then he wanted to see you, so we pulled you out."

"And it's good you did," said Bess. "Harry never carries a lock pick with him. I always have them and pass them to him. Sometimes in a kiss, other times by hand. It all depends on the situation."

"So, could you maybe pass him one now so I could get out of here?" asked Diana.

"Let me see the lock," said Harry as he walked towards the door and examined it.

"Can you open it?" asked Diana.

"I can try, but padlocks and handcuffs are my specialty. A door lock like this is one I've never seen before. Still, it can't hurt to try."

Bess passed Harry a few small pieces of metal and Diana watched in fascination as he inserted them and probed the interior of the lock. She expected the lock to fly open at any moment, but soon found herself fearing the worst as Harry rose with the door still locked.

"Odd," said Harry. "I can feel the pins and manipulate them into the right place then apply torque to the cylinder. The cylinder wants to move but the lock refuses to budge. It's as if there's a second mechanism that must be dealt with, but I have no clue what that is. I fear that I have failed you. This is a lock quite unlike any I've seen before."

"Dang!" muttered Diana. "I guess I'll just have to wait until morning then when the librarian shows up."

"I do want to thank you for reuniting me with my wife however," said Harry embracing Bess once more. He turned to Don Quixote and asked, "You said we could learn to leave the book ourselves?"

"You may already be able to simply by knowing you can. If not, I'll pull you out a time or two more and you'll get the hang of it."

"I hope so," said Harry.

"I suspect you'll get the hang of it pretty quickly," said Diana. "People seem to pop out pretty easily."

"I'm sorry again I couldn't help you," said Harry as he and his wife walked back into the bookshelves for some privacy.

"So, when does the librarian show up?" asked Diana.

"In just a few more hours," said Don Quixote. "I have to make sure everyone's tucked away in their books and the place is as she left it before she returns however, so I won't be here with you when she shows."

"Does she know about you all and what you can do?"

"No. You're the only human who knows of our abilities. We'd prefer you keep it that way. Perhaps you should try to get some sleep before she arrives. You must be getting quite tired."

"Yeah. Let me find where I put my flip flops and then maybe I will lie down for a bit."

"I believe they were atop the table over there."

"I thought so too, but they aren't there now," said Diana looking still more confused.

A search was started with Arthur, Cleopatra and Don Quixote looking around the space for them, but they were gone.

"That's weird," said Diana. "Who would steal some dollar store flip flops?"

"I know just the man to solve this mystery," said Don Quixote. "I'll be right back."

He disappeared into the book racks and emerged with a shortish man dressed impeccably who was brushing some dust from the sleeve of his jacket. A neatly trimmed mustache framed his mouth.

"Don Quixote, you simply must dust my book before pulling me out of it. This level of filth is most unacceptable."

"I'm sorry my old friend, but your services are needed. There has been a theft. This is the victim, Diana."

"It is a pleasure to meet you my dear," said the man with a twinkle in his eye. "I am Hercule Poirot. World renowned detective. I place myself at your service. What is it that was stolen? A priceless necklace? Gems? Perhaps a work of art?"

"My flip flops actually."

"Flip flops?"

"They're kind of like a sandal, only made of rubber," explained Diana.

"Ah, not the most impressive theft, but still, all thieves should be caught and held accountable regardless of the crime. It's time to dust off the little grey cells in my head and figure out what happened here."

"Do you think you can find them?"

"My dear girl, have no fear. Order and method will lead us to the perpetrator in no time. Let's start with the facts. Where were the flip flops when they were stolen?"

"On top of that table over there."

"And who was in the area at the time?"

"Don Quixote, Arthur, Cleopatra, Romeo, and Harry and his wife Bess. Others were brought out for a few seconds but then went back into their books."

"Do we know exactly when they were stolen?"

"Not really."

"I see. No timeline complicates matters, but no fear. I've solved tougher cases before. Can you rule out anyone as the thief?"

"Don Quixote has pretty much been by my side the whole time. I doubt it was him."

"It was not," said Hercule. "I've known that man for quite some time now and had he taken them his chivalrous nature would force him to confess. Arthur seems an unlikely suspect. These flip flops were women footwear you say?"

"Yes."

"And we have two women remaining as suspects. Most interesting."

"You can rule me out," said Cleopatra who'd been observing from the side. "I've already got a superior pair of sandals."

"This other woman, this Bess was it? What do we know of her?"

"She's Harry Houdini's wife."

"The escape artist? The man who could escape from any pair of handcuffs? That felon?"

"I'm not sure I'd call him a felon," said Diana.

"Any man who makes his living escaping from police custody is a felon in my eyes," said Hercule. "A man of such reputation would likely think little of stealing a pair of these flip flop things."

"I was with them pretty much from the time they emerged though and I'm pretty sure I'd have noticed if they had my flip flops. Whoever did it likely did it while I wasn't watching."

"And when would that have been?"

"Maybe when we were looking for the door key in the office or when Don Quixote was taking me through the aisles of books."

"Where was everyone when you were in the office?"

"They were all with me. Cleopatra was standing in the doorway, while Arthur and Don Quixote helped me search."

"And this Harry Houdini and his wife?"

"They hadn't been pulled from their books yet."

"And where was Romeo during this time?" asked Hercule.

"He started following us then got a little too intimate with Cleopatra and she sent him off to the book racks."

"And what was he doing there?" asked Hercule. "Looking for something to read?"

"He pulled one of the prostitutes from les Miserables to have sex with," said Cleopatra. "He does that sort of thing fairly frequently."

"And with what did he pay the girl, one wonders?" asked Hercule turning his eye towards Romeo who'd been staying largely in the background.

"My good company?" suggested Romeo.

"I've been around you boy. Your good company would not buy much. Tell me the truth. Did you steal the flip flops for your whore?"

"I prefer to think of it more as a borrow. She couldn't take them back into the book with her since they weren't in the book originally."

"So, where are they now?"

"Behind the book on the shelf," said Romeo. "She placed them there so she could have them the next time she came out. She said they were exquisite."

"As I promised my dear," said Hercule Poirot to Diana. "The case has been solved. Don Quixote, I trust you'll return the flip flops to the girl?"

"I'll go get them now," said Don Quixote as he turned and walked into the book aisle.

"My dear girl, if you ever have need of me again, do not hesitate to call for my services. Now if you'll excuse me, I must return to my book. I was pulled away from a most fascinating case."

"Thank you for your help," said Diana as Hercule bowed and walked away, passing Don Quixote as he carried the now recovered flip flops back to Diana.

"Here they are my lady."

"Thank you so much for the help. This has been a very strange night for me. I've learned a lot, but I still think I might be a bit insane. It's amazing hearing your stories."

"Ah, but you've but heard the tip of the iceberg when it comes to our stories. Much of our lives remains unwritten."

"You know stuff that wasn't written?"

"Indeed," said Don Quixote. "Some of it was edited out, some of it just a brief flash in the mind of our writer, but there is so much more to us than is on the printed page. In the hands of the right author so much more could be done with each of our stories."

"Interesting. I'd assumed what was written was all there was."

"He's right," said Arthur. "There are countless stories of battles won and lost. Loves lost and found within each of us that never made it to paper. What you've read and heard to date is but a fraction of who we are."

"What happens if something happens to a book that's here?"

"If a book is lost, so too are its characters," said Arthur. "When we get checked out, we lose our ability to leave the page. Don Quixote thinks there's some sort of a hive type behavior where we need to be together in a large enough mass to emerge successfully. I don't know if that's true or not, but I know I cannot leave my page on the rare occasion I'm checked out until I'm returned to be among the rest."

"Is it the location?"

"I think not. When we are checked out in multiples you can feel the bonds of the paper weakening, but when we are separated, the bonds are stronger and trap us to the page. I fear we must leave you now. Daylight is approaching and with it the return of the librarian. You should try to lie down and get some sleep. We shall go back to our books. It's been a pleasure meeting you fair Diana."

"The pleasure was all mine. Truly it was."

"Do you still question your sanity?"

"A bit perhaps, but not as much as I did earlier."

"Why is that?"

"I have this bizarre belief that everything in life happens for a reason and I think I might now know the reason this all happened."

"And what would that be?"

"I think I'm destined to be a hero of sorts."

"And a worthy one at that," said Arthur. "Now we must go. Goodbye Diana."

"Goodbye Arthur."

And the characters melted back into their books as Diana laid down on the cool carpet once more and thought of what she'd learned. It was nearly an hour later when she heard the key enter the lock and saw the librarian opening the door. She rose to greet the librarian.

"My goodness!" shouted the librarian. "You scared me. What are you doing here?"

"I'm afraid I fell asleep under that table yesterday and when I woke up the door was locked. I looked around for a key, but there was none."

"Are you okay? Are you hungry or thirsty?"

"No. I'm fine. Better than fine actually."

"What did you do here all night?"

"Oh, I just leafed through a few books and met a few of the characters. They're quite remarkable. I'm sorry if I scared you."

"Are you sure you're okay? Would you like me to drive you someplace?"

"Our cabin's just a short walk away. You have a lovely library."

"Had, I'm afraid. Today's my last day here. I just stopped by this morning to pick up a few things and clean out my desk."

"I'm sorry to hear that."

"Ah well, no one cares about old books these days anyway."

"I do."

"You're one of the few who do if that's true."

"I never used to but I kind of fell in love with them recently. It's almost like they've become friends. I'd better get going. My parents will be realizing I'm gone soon. I might just be able to sneak back in without them knowing I was gone all night."

The germ of an idea that had formed in Diana's head grew stronger and stronger with each step back towards the pair of cabins. She could see movement in the Gunderson's cabin and walked right past her parent's cabin to it and knocked on the door.

Mr. Gunderson opened the door.

"Debra is it?" asked Mr. Gunderson.

"Diana, actually."

"Sorry, it's early yet and I haven't had my caffeine to jumpstart my brain. Is something wrong?"

"I hear that you bought the old library."

"I did. The crew will show up later this week to tear it down. Then we'll start building new cabins. Pretty soon everything from the intersection to here will be cabins just like these."

"What are you going to do with the books?"

"I called some people about buying them, but the book dealers all said they were worthless. They'd charge me to haul them away. I'll just have the demo guys scoop them up with the rest of the debris and haul them to the landfill. I'd considered burning them to save the weight, but I'd need a permit for that and it's just not worth the trouble."

"Could I buy them from you?"

"Why? They're all old and pretty much no one cares for the old stories in them. From what I've heard you're not much of a reader."

"I found the library yesterday and fell asleep inside and spent the night there with the books. I'll gladly buy them if you'll just give me a good price."

"They're yours. Take them. It's that much less junk I have to haul to the landfill."

"Seriously?"

"Sure. You'll need a truck to haul them all away though. I've got a truck and a couple of guys coming around tomorrow who can take them back to your place though if you really want them. They're taking the reusable furniture and whatnots back to the city for me, so they can haul the books for you if you'd like also."

"That would be fantastic! Just be careful with them."

"I'll have them boxed up and delivered to your house. Have you asked your parents if it's okay?"

"Not yet, but we've got a big empty basement where I can put them for now."

"How about I have my guys bring the racks too? You can keep them organized that way."

"That would be amazing!"

"Did you really sleep there all night? Sorry about that. Your parents must be worried to death."

"I doubt they even know I'm missing. I'm heading there now. Thanks again."

PART TWO

Seventy years had passed since Diana spent the night in that small library. Those years were quite unlike any she could have ever imagined before that night. By the end of her senior year in high school she'd self-published her first modern adaptation of a classic. It was the story of King Arthur, told from the perspective of Guinevere. After a slow start, sales had built and gotten the attention of a mainstream publisher who offered her a publishing deal. In the years since then she'd published sixty-five such adaptations, each selling well.

Fame as a writer was never something she wanted. She stayed true to herself and never moved to New York City or Los Angeles. She bought a large plot of land in South Jersey and built a large home. Well, in truth the home portion was small, but it was built around a massive private library. Her rare trips out of her home were often to used bookstores where she'd nearly empty the shelves. Her home library grew to hold well in excess of a million books. She was known in the media as a reclusive writer, largely devoid of friends.

When she'd become pregnant at age forty, it had come as a surprise to nearly everyone. Her agent, publicist and publisher had all been surprised. Inquiries into the identity of the father had gone nowhere as she'd only say it was an old friend and they'd simply spent one night together. She'd say no more. When the child was born, Diana legally changed her last name to Montague, but never wed. Her daughter Gwen had no interest in writing or books and often joked that her mother cared for the books more than her.

Their relationship, as was true of many mother/daughter relationships, had been challenging. Gwen was outgoing and daring while her mother had become more and more reclusive over the years. Loud arguments between the pair were not uncommon, though few doubted their love for one another. Gwen had left home in her late teen years, married, had a child named Julie, gotten divorced, married again, got divorced again, then died in an auto accident. Diana had then finished raising her granddaughter.

As is often the case, the skipped generation between the Diana and her granddaughter made their relationship smoother. It helped that both Diana and her granddaughter shared a passion for the written word. Her granddaughter had studied literature at the university and had laughed when she saw that one of her courses was on her grandmother's writings. The fact that she had nearly failed the course was something both she and Diana found very amusing.

Julie's degree and name had earned her an invitation to work for her grandmother's publisher right out of college. To the shock and amazement of her friends, she'd declined the offer, and decided to focus on writing instead. She'd returned to her childhood home only to discover that Diana's health had declined. The immune-based cancer treatments were failing, and Diana was dying. Julie went from aspiring writer, to dedicated caregiver.

Dr. Carroll had been to see her grandmother and had just left when Julie was called to Diana's bedside where she found her sitting on the edge of the bed.

"What did the doctor say?" asked Julie, already knowing the news from the briefing the doctor gave her on his way out.

"That it's time to make sure my affairs are in order," said Diana.

"As they are. Your lawyers have seen to that. Everything is settled and there's nothing left to do."

"There is one thing. If you wouldn't mind taking me to the library, there's something I need to show you."

"I can get you anything you want from the library rather than you have to go down there," offered Julie.

"Not this you can't," said Diana with a sly smile. "You have to see this yourself."

Julie pulled the wheelchair over and helped her grandmother into the chair then wheeled her down the hallway to the recently installed elevator to take her to the library. She wheeled her out of the elevator and into the center of the library.

"Now, what is it I have to see?"

"Not what, but who. People say I've lived a solitary life, but they've never been more wrong. They say I'm dying friendless, but once again they're wrong. I'd like you to meet my friends. They've been those closest to me over the last seventy years and quite frankly I don't know what I'd have done without them. Don Quixote, if you don't mind, could you show yourself to my granddaughter?"

"Did Dr. Carroll give you more pain medicine?" asked Julie wondering about her grandmother's mental state.

Before Diana could answer Julie heard a faint clinking sound getting louder and louder and looked up to see a knight in armor walking towards them.

"Who are you?"

"I'm Don Quixote de la Mancha," said the knight. "A trusted friend of your grandmother for these past seventy years. In fact, I owe my very existence to her. Without her I would have been destroyed back then."

"What is this?"

"My dear girl," said Diana placing a hand on Julie's arm. "What do I tell every interviewer when they ask me what inspired me to write my stories?"

"That the characters spoke to you."

"And they do. This is Don Quixote. One of the many characters here who has spoken to me through the years and possibly the most powerful of the lot."

Diana turned to Don Quixote and nodded and asked, "Could you send out the rest?"

"As you wish my lady."

Characters now streamed from the aisles between bookshelves and formed a circle around the pair with many coming up and touching Diana affectionately, some with tears in their eyes at seeing her in this state. Warm words were exchanged between them and Diana.

"Don Quixote, Arthur, King of the Britons and Cleopatra, Queen of the Nile were among those to first interact with me."

Julie stared around at everyone in amazement and slowly shook her head.

"I know how you feel meeting them for the first time," said Diana. "But my time is running short and I felt you should meet."

"Trust me, you have no idea how strange this feels."

"I can assure you I do. Or, did once anyway. You'll question your sanity for a bit, but gradually come to accept the reality."

"The reality?"

"They are real. They can exist in human form. It takes years, fifty or more, but they can then be pulled from the pages and exist outside their books."

"I think I'm losing my mind."

"She truly is related to you," said Arthur offering a chair for Julie to sit in as she started to wobble on her feet. "Your grandmother refused to accept our existence for quite some time. She felt she was going insane. Even Dr. Freud coming out to talk to her did little to reassure her."

"Dr. Freud?" asked Julie.

"Sigmund Freud, and yes, that Sigmund Freud," said Diana. "He's likely in the crowd here somewhere if you'd like to meet him. If he didn't come out, then Don Quixote can pull him out if you'd like to meet him."

"No. I'm not sure there's anything he could say to help me understand this."

"I probably should have introduced you to them earlier when your mind was still more open to new ideas, but I opted not to. I'm sorry about that."

Julie looked around the room at the hundreds of characters who'd emerged seemingly from nowhere and then looked back to Diana.

"They're real? You can touch them?"

"And more. I never told your mother who her father, your grandfather was. I knew she'd never understand."

"He's one of them?"

"Romeo, Romeo, wherefore art thou Romeo," called out Diana.

"I am here my lady."

"I want you to meet your granddaughter, and you must promise to keep your hands off this one."

"Even I have some morals," said Romeo.

"Hah!" sneered Cleopatra and several other women in the crowd.

"He's a kid!" muttered Julie.

"He's a five hundred plus year old sixteen-year-old if you want to get technical about it," said Diana

"And you slept with him?"

"I was having a bad day. I know it's no excuse, but he wore me down. It was just the once and frankly I had no clue I could get pregnant from a fictional character. It was quite the surprise."

"I'll bet. Have you slept with any of the others?"

"No. Our relationship is more business than personal. I protect them and they help me write their stories. That's why I called you down here tonight. My time here is passing, and they'll need your protection. They also have many more stories to tell and while you're a good writer, they can make you a better one."

"I don't know. I just don't understand."

"If it's any help I'll be here too, to help you and guide you."

"How?"

"In one of my early works I included myself in the story. Critics of the time and your college professor called it a vanity move. It was more than that. It was a way to ensure my immortality. Don Quixote has assured me that the character version of me is nearly ready to be pulled from the pages. Within a few days or weeks, I'll be free to rejoin you, only in a younger form, despite my passing from this life. I included your mother in a work shortly after you were born. She has farther to go yet, but she too will join us down the road. Every day new characters ripen and are ready to be pulled from their pages. This space was made to accommodate them.

"My architect and builder could not understand why I built such a large library with such small personal spaces. It is because this library was to become my home as it is the home for so many of my dear friends."

"These characters are your friends?"

"Indeed, Cleopatra is one of my oldest and dearest friends and she's agreed to help ease me on my way out of the world. My death need not be painful or unduly unpleasant. The pain meds barely help me now. I can feel the cancer eating away at me. My life is measured more in hours or days than weeks. It's time for me to move on.

"The poison her asp possesses is not one that's screened for and the small puncture wounds he makes will not be noticed. All will assume I died of cancer, as it is what is truly killing me. But with you now learning of this and being introduced to my friends, my mission here is done. It is time for you to take over. It's time I found an end to the pain. Listen to their stories and let them help you write new tales featuring them. I've barely scratched the surface of what can be done."

"This is crazy," muttered Julie. "This can't be true."

"It is my dear. It truly is. My time is done. Cleopatra and I will end things now. If you wish to stay you can. The same goes for everyone here. But it's time to end this chapter of the book. My new chapter will be starting in a few days so long as Don Quixote and the rest are kept safe. I can't guarantee that I'll recognize you when I come back but give me time to adjust and I will do my best to guide you along the way. Do you have any last words for Granny?"

"I don't want you to go!"

"And I would prefer not to leave, but it's my time. I will be back soon though. Don Quixote will guide you until I return. He's a bit mad, but in a good way. Cleo my dear. You've offered to let me hold your asp many times and I've refused. I am now ready."

"So be it, my friend."

Cleopatra handed the asp to Diana who pressed it against her arm and felt the small needle-like fangs dig in. She handed the asp back then closed her eyes and drifted off. Julie sat there in tears as one by one the friends of her grandmother paraded past, patting her on the shoulder and crying themselves at the loss of their friend.

"She's in a better place," said Cleopatra as one of the last to return to the shelves.

Soon, only Don Quixote remained.

"My lady, if you need anything, you need only call for me and I'll come running. Your grandmother was a dear friend to me, and I owe her my very existence. As do most of us here. We will do anything we can for you. You owe us nothing in return."

Julie simply nodded her head as she wiped the tears from her face and watched as Don Quixote moved back into the shelves. She was now alone. She checked Diana's pulse but there was none. She appeared to have just drifted off peacefully while sitting in the chair. Julie pulled out her cellular phone and made the first of many calls to inform those necessary of the passing of her grandmother.

The funeral took place four days later. Only those closest to Diana had been invited to attend. The crowd was very small with just her publicist, editor, agent and a representative from the publishing house also in attendance.

Her grandmother's agent offered his condolences to Julie and remarked, "It's just a shame she had so few friends. She was a remarkable woman."

Julie wiped away a tear and smiled before replying, "She had her books."

It was nearly three weeks later when Don Quixote advised Julie that her grandmother's character was now ready to emerge. Julie watched in amazement as he reached into the book and extracted her grandmother in a younger form.

"Welcome home," said Julie embracing the confused looking woman. "Welcome home."

AUTHOR NOTES

I hope you liked reading this silly little story that popped into my head over a couple of days. It was one of those stories that largely wrote itself. Please feel free to post reviews of the story online at Amazon, Goodreads or any other site you frequent. Word of mouth is the best thing an author has going for him/her these days. If you liked this story you might like some of my other books, all available at Amazon.

Another short story I wrote is "[Becoming Santa](#)". It tells the tale of a young teen-aged boy who suddenly starts seeing visions of Santa Claus wherever he goes. He fears he's losing his mind, but soon learns otherwise.

My 2012 Amazon Breakthrough Novel Award Semi-finalist "[The Campaign,](#)" described by Publishers' Weekly (in draft form) as a "fun romp" and "a winner," tells the story of a small advertising firm that stumbles into creating a popular Super Bowl ad then finds that recapturing that success isn't quite so easy a second time around. It's got a fun cast including the Lawrence Olivier of pig actors in Mr. Pinky and his pig-like owner Mrs. Perkins.

On a more serious noted, in "To Rise or Fall" Dr. Jerry Rusk discovers to his great shock and amazement that the new general anesthetic compound he's testing lets those undergoing anesthesia with it, visit the afterlife they've earned up to that time. For those who rise, the experience is something they want to repeat again and again. For those who fall, they emerge determined to change their ways after seeing what now awaits them in the afterlife. Things get kind of interesting when a televangelist and politicians start using the anesthetic.

In "Annie's Gift" a teen-aged girl receives an inheritance from a grandmother she thought had died years earlier, only to learn that she'd just died recently. The gift is a very large, very old book, that oddly enough appears to be filled with all blank pages. Her mother demands she gets rid of it, so she takes it to a used book dealer who works with Annie to try and unravel the mystery of the book. Then magically the pages of the book refill when an older man enters the bookstore and then disappears when he leaves. Annie soon discovers a whole new world where a sleeping fire breathing dragon is slowly awakening. Unlike dragons of lore, this one doesn't breathe fire out, but in, absorbing its energy and growing more and more powerful. Soon, only Annie stands between the dragon and the end of the world. There's just one problem. She doesn't know what to do to stop it.

In "Josh Saves the Planet" Josh is a member of the Earth Defense Force having inherited his grandfather's spacecraft that's been passed down in is family for generations. When a foreign exchange student enters his life, his world turns upside down. It turns out she may be a tad more foreign than he'd thought. With an invading force of giant bunny-like creatures coming, Josh is the only thing between them and the loss of the planet. Just a note here. This story was inspired when I commented on the old ABNA (Amazon Breakthrough Novel Award) forums that I was tired of aliens always being reptilian or shiny silver beings. Why not a giant bunny or something? It was suggested I write a book featuring giant bunny aliens, so I did.

In book one of the "Sara X" series we meet Sara who is a wife and mother and former professional assassin who specialized in making deaths appear natural. When a former client of hers finds himself in line to become president, Sara's knowledge of what he'd paid her to do becomes an issue for him. His father-in-law, Roger Bentley, founder of Bentley Security arranges to have Sara killed. There's just one problem. They missed and killed her husband and son instead. Now Sara is on the warpath and God help anyone who gets in her way. "Sara X" was picked to be in Jason Chen's Political Thriller Story Bundle back in 2016.

In book two of the series, "Sara X, A Broken Trust" Sara is hired to take out Benjamin Schwartz, a politician now running for president who's gaining support and has access to data stolen from the Hasselberg Group that could be very damaging if revealed. Concerned about how much Sara knows of them they've also got another assassin in place to remove Sara. Instead of killing Schwartz, Sara ends up allying with Schwartz and creating chaos for the members of the Hasselberg Group.

And for those thinking of building a new house, my one nonfiction book "How To Save Money On Your New Home" looks into some of the design decisions that can drastically affect the cost of your new home and where it's wiser to spend money now versus later. Things like the footprint of the home can change the cost of building a home dramatically.

More new books are on the way including the third in the "Sara X" series, another shorter story called "Project GEE" that's a lot of fun and should be out shortly. In Project GEE a physicist finds that by determining the exact state of an atom at two separate times he can recreate everything that occurred in between those two measurements. This leads to a confrontation between him and the CIA where an unlikely group of heroes comes to his rescue.

And a dystopian novel set in the future where the powers-that-be have decided no human can read more than ten thousand books in a lifetime and they create a list of the ten thousand books that can be read, while banning all others. The story is called "**The Ten Thousand**" and follows a young boy who is discovered to have a writing talent. He's sent to a special government backed writing school and university where his first novel makes the list of the ten thousand. Then he finds a hidden library filled with banned books and old news accounts of what had really happened and not the government backed version. His awakening to the truth of what really happened creates an interesting set of problems for him and his friends.

Thanks again for reading this story and please do post a review if you can. A new book should be appearing every few months as I finalize them and get the covers done.

Made in United States
North Haven, CT
23 November 2025